Backyard SPORTS™

Hand-Off

By Michael Teitelbaum

Illustrated by Ron Zalme

Grosset & Dunlap • A Stonesong Press Book

A Stonesong Press Book

GROSSET & DUNLAP
Published by the Penguin Group
Penguin Group (USA) Inc., 375 Hudson Street, New York, New York 10014, USA
Penguin Group (Canada), 90 Eglinton Avenue East, Suite 700,
Toronto, Ontario M4P 2Y3, Canada
(a division of Pearson Penguin Canada Inc.)
Penguin Books Ltd., 80 Strand, London WC2R 0RL, England
Penguin Group Ireland, 25 St. Stephen's Green, Dublin 2, Ireland
(a division of Penguin Books Ltd.)
Penguin Group (Australia), 250 Camberwell Road, Camberwell,
Victoria 3124, Australia
(a division of Pearson Australia Group Pty. Ltd.)
Penguin Books India Pvt. Ltd., 11 Community Centre, Panchsheel Park,
New Delhi—110 017, India
Penguin Group (NZ), 67 Apollo Drive, Rosedale, North Shore 0632,
New Zealand (a division of Pearson New Zealand Ltd.)
Penguin Books (South Africa) (Pty.) Ltd., 24 Sturdee Avenue,
Rosebank, Johannesburg 2196, South Africa

Penguin Books Ltd., Registered Offices: 80 Strand, London WC2R 0RL, England

Library of Congress Control Number: 2008013365

ISBN 978-0-448-44900-5   10 9 8

Chapter One

Pablo Sanchez dashed out onto the football field. He had been waiting for this day for months, and it was finally football season. He was so psyched to be playing as he and his friends gathered on the field for their first practice of the season.

"Hi, Joey!" Pablo shouted as he joined his flag football teammates Joey MacAdoo, Samantha "Sam" Pearce, Tony Delvecchio, Ernie Steele, and Vicki Kawaguchi.

"Welcome to the team, dude!" Tony said, giving Pablo a high five. "Glad you decided to join us this year."

Pablo was a natural athlete. He loved

playing baseball, basketball, and soccer with his friends.

He also loved football. He always watched pro and college games on TV. But he had always been too busy playing other sports during football season to join his friends' football team. Finally, this year, he had decided to play with his friends.

"I couldn't miss another season," Pablo said. "I really want to play, and I'm ready to help this team!"

"We're happy you're here, Pabs," Joey said.

"Yeah, it's a lot more fun to be on the field, right in the middle of the action, than it is to watch it on TV," Ernie added. "And no one is more in the middle than me. I'm the center!"

With that, Ernie bent over, grabbed the ball, and snapped it back through his legs. The ball shot right into Joey's waiting hands. Joey was the team's quarterback.

"Vicki, go deep!" Joey shouted as he dropped back a few steps. He uncorked a perfect spiral. The ball arced through the air toward Vicki, who raced downfield. She reached out without breaking her stride and caught the ball over her shoulder.

"I could be a wide receiver like Vicki," Pablo announced enthusiastically. "Or a running back. Or a lineman, or a defensive back, or—"

"Hey, we all know you're fast, Pablo," Ernie interrupted. "But even you can only play one position at a time."

Pablo laughed. He was so excited to finally be playing that he was ready to do everything all at once.

"Why don't we start off with some basics," Joey said, handing Pablo a belt. Two small flags, one on each side, were attached to the belt with Velcro. "The game is pretty much the same as the pros play. You get four downs to go ten yards. If you make it, you get a new set of downs, and so on. Touchdowns are still six points, if you kick the extra point it's one, and if you kick a field goal it's three. The big difference is that in flag football, instead of tackling the person with the ball, the defense pulls a flag off his or her belt. Like this." Joey reached out and snatched a flag from Pablo's belt.

"Got it," Pablo said confidently, pressing the flag back into place.

"Okay, great," Joey said. "Let's try a simple pass pattern, Pablo. Nothing fancy, just run about ten yards then cut sharply to the sideline. I'll throw you the ball there."

"Great," Pablo said, then he set up a few feet to the left of Ernie.

"I'll cover you," shouted Sam as she ran out to her position as a defensive back. She faced Pablo.

"Take it easy on the new kid, Sam!" Tony yelled. Everyone laughed. Pablo may have been new to football, but his friends all knew what a great athlete he was.

Ernie snapped the ball and Pablo bolted off the line of scrimmage. When he had run about ten yards, Pablo planted his right foot and cut quickly to his left. Sam stayed with him.

As Pablo approached the left sideline, Joey fired a lead pass to him that was right on target. The ball landed in Pablo's hands.

"Nice," Joey said. "Good speed, good cut, and good hands."

"You know, making that cut was kind of like the moves I make in basketball or soccer to get free," Pablo explained as he trotted back toward Joey.

"And those magic hands of yours that scoop up grounders at shortstop don't hurt either," Ernie added.

He'd only run one play, but Pablo was sure that football would be just as much fun as he had hoped.

"Let's practice some hand-offs," Joey suggested.

Everyone except Ernie lined up behind Joey. Ernie stayed at center so he could snap the ball to Joey for this drill.

One by one, each player took a hand-off from Joey and ran straight ahead. When it was Pablo's turn, Joey paused and turned to his friend.

"The hand-off is a real basic part of the game, and it looks simple," Joey explained. "But it's the place where lots of fumbles occur, so the fundamentals are really important."

"I'm ready," Pablo said excitedly.

"Okay, place your right arm across your chest," Joey began. "Then put your left arm across your belly. I'm going to pop the ball right in between. As soon as I do, close up your arms and hug the ball tightly. Got it?"

"Got it," Pablo replied as he set up his arms exactly as Joey had described.

Joey took the snap from Ernie, spun around, and handed the ball off to Pablo. Pablo clutched the ball firmly and ran straight ahead, just as his teammates had done before him.

"Pabs, you're a natural," Joey said, smiling, as Pablo flipped the ball back to him. "Let's work on some blocking fundamentals."

Joey, Ernie, and Sam lined up as the offensive line, facing Vicki, Tony, and Pablo who were set up on the defensive line.

"Okay, remember, on offense, you can't use your hands to grab the player you're blocking," Joey explained. "Keep them close to your body and put yourself in between the defensive lineman and the quarterback! On defense, use your hands to push the offensive lineman out of the way, but don't grab the uniform. If you're bigger than the person you're blocking, use your size. If not, use your speed."

Pablo was lined up facing Ernie who was much taller.

"Ready!" Joey called out. "Block!"

Pablo took one quick step forward. As

Ernie tried to use his size to push Pablo out of the way, Pablo took a quick step to his right, then sped back to the left and ran past Ernie.

Ernie turned around. "Joey didn't really mean for you to beat me, Pablo, when he said that stuff about using your speed," he joked. Pablo laughed.

The team ran through a few more drills, some running plays, pass patterns, and practicing hand-offs again.

"Okay, good practice everyone," Joey shouted. "Let's take a lap and wrap it up for today."

Everyone started jogging around the field.

"So what did you think of your first practice, rookie?" Tony asked Pablo as he ran beside him.

"Football is awesome, Tony," Pablo replied. "I was nervous I wouldn't do well, but it seems like football was made for me. I can't wait until we play for real!"

"You won't have long to wait," Sam pointed out as she jogged along. "We've got a game against Pete, Dante, and a bunch of those guys tomorrow."

"And that's when we unleash our new secret weapon," Ernie added.

"What's that?" Pablo asked.

"You, Pablo!" Vicki exclaimed. "You're our secret weapon!"

"Secret weapon," Pablo said, thinking about how much he was looking forward to the next day's game. "I like the sound of that!"

As the team completed their lap and practice wrapped up, Joey pulled a thick loose-leaf binder from his backpack and handed it to Pablo.

"What's this?" Pablo asked. He needed two hands to hold the heavy book.

"That's our playbook," Joey explained. "You need to study it before the game."

"You mean, like homework?" Pablo asked.

"Yeah, except there's no pop quiz the next day," Joey replied smiling. "Football isn't just played on the field, you know."

"Joey's right," Ernie said, laughing. "Sometimes, when it rains, we play in my basement."

"What Joey means," Vicki began, playfully punching Ernie in the arm, "is that we all have to study and learn the plays."

"No problem, Joey," Pablo said, feeling great about his first football practice. "See you at the game tomorrow."

That evening Pablo did his schoolwork, ate his dinner, and watched a little TV. Just before it was time to go to bed, he flipped open the huge playbook Joey had given to him.

Here's that pass pattern I tried in

practice, he thought. *That was pretty easy. And here are some basic running plays. This stuff doesn't look too hard.*

As Pablo continued turning pages he came to some plays that he hadn't practiced. *Hmm . . . these look kind of complicated. Out route, post pattern, fly, reverse, hook, slant . . . We didn't get that far along in practice. I guess the team isn't using these yet.*

He closed the book. *I know the basics,* he thought, yawning. *I'll be fine tomorrow— they didn't call me the secret weapon for nothing!*

Then he flipped off his light and slipped into bed.

Chapter Two

Pablo took a deep breath as he settled
into his position as the running back.
He lined up in the backfield, directly
behind Joey, the quarterback. Pablo felt
ready for his first game of six-on-six flag
football against a bunch of kids from their
neighborhood.

Sam and Tony set themselves on the
offensive line, on either side of Ernie, the
center. Vicki trotted a few yards to the
right of Tony, taking her position as wide
receiver.

Ernie bent over and placed his hands on
the ball. As Joey stepped up, ready for the

snap, Pablo repeated the play to himself one more time.

Joey hands off to me and I run through the hole between Ernie and Tony. Pablo knew what he had to do; he was ready to play.

Joey glanced to his right at Vicki, then back over his shoulder at Pablo. "Green-21-green-21. Hut-hut-hut."

On the third "hut" Ernie snapped the ball back, placing it into Joey's waiting hands. Joey spun around as Pablo drove forward. Tony blocked his man, Pete, chest-high, forcing him to the right. At the same time, Ernie straightened up after the snap and pushed Dante, another defensive lineman, to the left.

The hole Pablo had hoped for was right there. All he had to do was run through it. Joey placed the ball firmly into his arms. Pablo gripped it tightly and raced toward the hole.

Trying to slip past the defense, Pablo came face-to-face with A.C., a linebacker for the other team. A.C. reached out and snatched the flag off of Pablo's belt.

"Gotcha!" A.C. shouted as Pablo slowed down and flipped the ball to Ernie. He had only picked up about a yard on the play.

These guys are quick! Pablo thought as he trotted back to the huddle.

"Okay, team, huddle up!" Joey shouted. "Second and nine," Joey announced to his teammates in the huddle. "Let's try a ten-yard curl pattern to Vicki. Pablo, you stay in the backfield to help give me some extra protection from the pass rush. Ready? On two. Break!"

A curl pattern? Pablo thought. *I don't remember seeing that in the playbook. Still, all I have to do on this play is block. I can do that.*

The team broke the huddle and Pablo set

up in the running-back position.

Man, those guys are big! Pablo thought as he stared at the defensive linemen he would have to block.

Joey leaned over center and started barking out signals. "Blue-32-blue-32. Hut-hut!"

Ernie snapped the ball.

As Joey dropped back to set up for the pass, Vicki raced downfield about ten yards. She was covered by Kiesha, the other team's defensive back. Vicki stopped suddenly and turned back toward Joey, running a classic curl pattern.

But behind the line of scrimmage

things were not going quite so well. Defensive lineman Reese slipped past Sam, who was supposed to be blocking him. This was exactly why Pablo was needed as an extra blocker.

Pablo stepped up to block Reese, but Reese spun right past him and snatched the flag off Joey's belt before he could throw the ball. The play resulted in a five-yard loss.

"Sorry, Joey," Pablo said. *These guys are really good!* he thought.

"Forget it, Pabs," Joey replied. "Next time try to stay in front of him no matter which way he turns. Okay, huddle up, guys!"

As Pablo joined his teammates in the huddle, he couldn't stop thinking about the fact that everyone else on the field was a lot better at football than he was.

His team now faced a third-and-fourteen situation. Joey called for Vicki to run an out pattern. On the play, she dashed upfield, then cut to the outside. Joey hit her with a

pinpoint pass, but she stepped out of bounds
short of the first down.

On fourth down, Tony punted. After
a short runback, Ricky, the other team's
quarterback, lined up with his team's
offense.

Pablo took his position as a linebacker
on defense. His job on a running play was
to stop a running back who got past the
defensive line. On a passing play, he had
to help Sam, the defensive back, cover
receivers.

Ricky barked out signals, then took the
snap and handed off to Pete, his running
back. With a slick move, Pete faked his
way past Tony and put on a burst of speed.
Pablo rushed up to meet him. Pete took a
quick step to his left. Pablo turned in that
direction and reached out to grab the flag on
Pete's belt.

But Pete cut sharply back to his

right and slipped away from Pablo. Vicki, the team's other linebacker, was backing up the play and managed to snag Pete's flag. But he had picked up twenty yards and a first down on the play.

Pablo gathered with his teammates in the defensive huddle. "Pabs, why don't you take a turn at defensive back," Joey suggested. "Your speed will help you there. Switch positions with Sam."

"Okay," Pablo said. He jogged over to his new position. He was trying to focus on what he had learned in practice. *Don't let the receiver get behind you*, he repeated to himself.

Dante, the other team's wide receiver, lined up facing Pablo. Ricky took the snap, and Dante streaked downfield in what appeared to be a classic fly pattern—run as fast as you can and try to get behind the defender.

But Pablo was fast and stayed with his man, step for step.

Realizing that he wasn't going to get past Pablo, Dante slowed down. He started to turn back toward the quarterback.

He's running a curl pattern like Vicki did before, Pablo thought, slowing down to stay with him.

That's when Dante turned back upfield, put on a burst of speed, and blew right past Pablo. Ricky launched a long bomb that Dante caught in stride. He dashed into the end zone for the first touchdown of the game.

As Dante's team traded high fives, Joey,

Ernie, and the others gathered around Pablo.

"You got fooled, dude!" Tony said, shaking his head. "You gotta look for that fake every time."

Pablo nodded. He felt horrible. The last thing he wanted to do was let his teammates down. *Why is this so hard?* he thought. *I'm good at every other sport. What's wrong with me?*

"Keep your head in the game, Pabs," Joey said as if he were reading Pablo's mind.

Following a successful extra point, Ricky's team kicked off, holding a 7–0 lead.

After the return, Joey leaned into the huddle. "Okay guys, we're going to get this touchdown back, and Pablo's going to do it for us."

"Okay," Pablo said, eager for a chance to make up for his mistake. *Come on. You can do this*, he thought, trying to psych himself up for the next play.

"We're going to pull off a gadget play," Joey explained.

Pablo froze. "A gadget play?" he asked, anxiously. He didn't recall reading about that one in the playbook.

"Yeah, a trick play," Joey continued. "Something unusual that they won't be expecting. We're going to try the old hook and ladder."

That one sounded sort of familiar to Pablo. Maybe he had glanced at it in the playbook. But he still had no clue as to what he was supposed to do.

"Um, I'm not sure I know that one, Joey," Pablo said sheepishly.

"It's in the playbook!" Joey said sharply. "I thought you read it."

"I guess I didn't get that far," Pablo replied, looking around. His teammates were all staring down at the ground. He could tell that they were disappointed in him.

"Okay, here it is," Joey began. "Vicki heads downfield and runs a hook pattern."

Pablo kept quiet about the fact that he had no idea what a hook pattern was.

"Pablo, you follow her, about five yards behind," Joey continued. "We're trying to make it look like the pass is going to you, but it's really going to Vicki. Then once she catches it, she'll toss a lateral to you. Got it?"

"Got it!" Pablo said quickly, although he wasn't really sure he had gotten it.

The team lined up and Joey called out the signals. "Red-44-red-44. Hut-hut-hut!"

Joey took the snap and dropped back to pass. Vicki sped down the field. Pablo dashed out of the backfield, staying about five yards behind Vicki.

She stopped suddenly and turned back.

Joey timed his pass perfectly, and the ball arrived in Vicki's arms just as she spun around. But the play was only half over.

Trailing Vicki the whole time, Pablo was now five yards behind her and off to her right. Once it became clear that the pass was going to Vicki and not Pablo, all the defenders raced toward her. Which was exactly what Joey had hoped for when he called the play.

Before anyone could grab Vicki's flag, she tossed a lateral pass, behind her and to her left. Perfect.

Or it would have been, if Pablo had been on her left. Unfortunately he was on her right. The ball hit the ground and Kiesha, who was covering Vicki, pounced on top of it. She recovered the fumble and got the ball back for her team.

"You're supposed to be on my left," Vicki said when they got back into the huddle.

"You would have had a wide open field. And with your speed you would have scored for sure."

Pablo didn't know what to say. He realized now that he should have studied the playbook a little harder. But he had no idea that his team was going to use such complicated plays in their first game. And now he had not only blown a chance to score, but it was his fault that the other team had the ball.

This has never happened to me before, he thought. *I'm usually one of the best guys out there, no matter what the sport!*

He saw his friends rolling their eyes and exchanging exasperated looks. They didn't have to say a word. He knew exactly what they were thinking. Pablo had let them down.

There was nothing he could do now except get ready to play defense. But even there, on play after play, he found himself in the wrong spot to defend against a pass or stop a running back.

With time running out, Joey and his teammates got the ball back. They gathered in the huddle. "Pablo, I think you should try being our wide receiver," he explained. "It's the best place for us to take advantage of your speed. Are you okay swapping positions, Vicki, and playing running back?"

"No problem," Vicki replied.

"Pablo, let's try a hook pass," Joey said. "Go out about ten yards then turn and hook back. I'll hit you as you turn."

"Okay," Pablo said, then he lined up against Kiesha. He tried to shake off the nervous feeling in his stomach.

Joey called out signals, then took the snap.

Pablo dashed ten yards in a straight line, then stopped and turned back.

Joey timed his pass perfectly. The ball was waiting for Pablo when he spun around. He grabbed it with both hands. But as he turned back upfield, Pablo lost control of the ball. It squirted loose, spun through the air, and landed right in Kiesha's hands.

She bolted forward, slipping past Pablo, then cut across the field, getting around Pablo's teammates who were desperately trying to grab one of her flags.

Vicki dove after her, reaching out to grab a flag, but she came up just short. Kiesha scooted into the end zone for another touchdown just as time ran out. Her team had won, 13–0.

Pablo felt horrible as his team huddled up. "It's all my fault we lost," Pablo said quietly. "I let the whole team down. I'll understand if you don't want me on your team after all."

"We want you on the team," Joey said. "But we also want you to be ready to play. What you need is extra practice. Tomorrow. Just you and me. We'll work on your moves and pass patterns. What do you say?"

"You know me, Joey," Pablo replied. "I'll work as hard as I can to get better. I'll see you tomorrow for practice." As he headed home, Pablo realized that he had a lot of catching up to do.

Chapter Three

That evening, Pablo sat in his room and studied his playbook. He started at page one and read each play carefully, memorizing the names and basic moves.

When he got to the more complicated plays, he pulled out a pad and pencil. He sketched out the route he would have to run on a pass play. He noted the blockers he would have to run between on a running play. And he did this

over and over, until the patterns stuck in his mind.

He read and wrote and memorized until he could barely keep his eyes open and he began to doze off. He closed the playbook and went to bed. But visions of hook patterns, curls, slants, and post patterns filled his dreams.

The next day Pablo arrived on the practice field twenty minutes before he was supposed to meet Joey. He pulled out the notes he had made the previous night and started studying again.

Reviewing the lines he had drawn showing the route of each pass pattern, Pablo dashed down the empty field, practicing each one. He cut sharply to his left, then to his right, and then slanted toward the goalpost.

"Well that's a first!" Joey exclaimed when he arrived a short while later. "I've never seen anyone practicing football alone!"

"Running these patterns helps me remember them, Joey," Pablo explained. "But I'm glad you're here. Even I'm not fast enough to throw a pass to myself!"

Joey laughed. "Okay, let's start off with some simple stuff," he said, holding the football. "Let's run a down-and-out. Did you get to that one in the playbook yet?"

"Yup," Pablo said proudly.

Pretending he had just received a snap, Joey dropped back. Pablo bolted forward, accelerating with each step. Then about ten yards up the field, he slowed down and cut sharply to his right, heading for the sideline. As Pablo made his cut, Joey threw the ball. It arced through the air and drifted down into Pablo's waiting hands. He caught the ball, then stepped out of bounds.

"Good one, Pabs," Joey said as Pablo trotted back and flipped the ball to his friend. "Try it again, only this time, try to make your cut without slowing down. You don't want to give the defender any time to figure out what you're doing."

"Okay, let's run it again," Pablo said enthusiastically.

Again, Joey dropped back and Pablo took off. This time he planted his left foot while still running full speed and made a sharp cut to the right. The ball was waiting for him and he made the catch.

"That's it!" Joey cried. "If you can make that cut while still going full speed, there's not a defender in the world who can stay with you, no matter how fast he is."

Pablo started to feel encouraged. "It feels easy when it's just you and me, Joey," Pablo pointed out. "I'm just a little nervous about letting you guys down in a real game."

"That's the trick, Pabs. Forget about everyone else," Joey suggested. "During a game, try to block out everything but the pattern you're running and catching the ball. There's nothing out there but you and me. Nothing else."

"Gotcha," Pablo said.

"Now let's try the same play but with a slightly different twist," Joey said. "Before you make your cut to the right, take a quick step to the left, like you're gonna cut that way. Then cut back to the right. If you can do it sharply enough, you'll have the defender leaning the wrong way. That will give you another step or two before he can recover. Plenty of time for me to get the ball to you."

Pablo broke from the line at top speed. Ten yards out he planted his right foot, took one step to the left, then cut back to the right. As he broke back he stumbled a bit, but recovered in time to catch the pass.

"Okay, Pabs, good start," Joey said. "But

you're taking a few little steps making the cut instead of one sharp step. Here, let me show you."

Joey flipped the ball to Pablo.

"You want me to throw?" Pablo asked anxiously.

"Sure!" Joey replied enthusiastically. "Why not? It's just practice."

"But I'm no quarterback, Joey," Pablo explained.

"Hey, what happened to the guy who said he's ready to play anywhere?" Joey asked.

"You're right," Pablo said smiling. "Now I'm a quarterback!"

Joey ran hard upfield for about fifteen yards. Then he cut sharply to his left.

As Joey made his cut, Pablo threw a pass to a point a few yards ahead of where Joey was. The ball rocketed through the air in a perfect spiral. Two steps later, Joey ran down the pass and caught it.

"Hey! Nice throw, Pabs!" Joey said, smiling as he ran back to Pablo. "You are a natural, man! Maybe you've found your true football calling!"

Pablo felt good about his throw. *That was pretty easy*, he thought. "Yeah, but we already *have* a quarterback!" He flipped the ball back to Joey.

"I know, but I just thought of another way to use that arm of yours," Joey said excitedly. "And we're going to use it in our next game. Tonight, really study the reverse in the playbook."

"The reverse," Pablo repeated, pulling out his notes and jotting it down.

"Now let's run the pass pattern again," Joey said.

The two friends practiced until it started getting dark. "I gotta get home, Pabs," Joey said. "You wanna walk with me?"

"I think I'll stay a while longer," Pablo replied.

"Sure," Joey said, seeing how seriously Pablo was taking football. "And don't worry. You'll be okay in the next game. See ya."

When Joey had left, Pablo went back to running pass patterns. Before he started each one, he shouted out the name of the play, as another way to help himself remember. Again and again he ran the plays, until it was really too dark to see where he was going. Then he finally headed home.

The next morning, Pablo sat at the breakfast table, studying his playbook. He absentmindedly nibbled on his toast as he flipped through the more complex plays.

"Pablo, come on. Finish your toast!" his mother insisted. "You'll be late for school!"

Pablo quickly finished his breakfast and then hurried to the bus stop, his playbook in hand.

As he waited for the school bus, he continued to read through the playbook.

HONK! HONK!

Pablo thought he heard a vague, annoying noise, but he ignored it. He was in the middle of studying the reverse play Joey had told him about and he didn't want to be disturbed.

HONK! HONK! HONK! HONK!

This time Pablo looked up. He saw the school bus sitting at the stop with its doors open.

"You planning on joining us anytime today?" the bus driver asked, shaking his head.

"What?" Pablo mumbled, then he suddenly realized that the whole bus was waiting for him. "Oh, sorry!" Then he hurried onto the bus.

That afternoon in the school lunchroom, Ernie sat down next to Pablo, placing his tray on the long table.

"Hey, Pabs, what you got there?" Ernie asked, seeing that Pablo was reading something very intently.

Pablo didn't respond. Ernie craned his neck to see the book Pablo was reading.

"Oh, it's our team playbook. Cool," Ernie said. "How's that going, huh? Pretty gripping stuff, right?"

Again Pablo said nothing.

"So, I guess you're getting all ready for our next game, huh?" Ernie asked. "Don't worry. We'll beat those guys this time. Hey, how'd your practice with Joey go?"

Pablo's face remained buried in his book. He was clearly oblivious to anything except the reverse play he was studying.

"Hey, Pablo, your nose is on fire!" Ernie cried.

But Pablo still didn't seem to notice that Ernie was there.

"Well, it's been really great having this little chat with you, Pabs," Ernie quipped. "We'll have to do it again real soon. There's nothing like a good lunch conversation. And this was nothing like a good lunch conversation."

Then Ernie got up.

Pablo looked up from the playbook. "Huh?" he said as Ernie started to walk away. "Did you say something, Ernie?"

Chapter Four

A few days later, Pablo and his friends
played another game against Ricky, Dante,
and their teammates.

As Pablo lined up at wide receiver he
thought of Joey's words. *It's just you and
me, Pabs.* He tried to block out everyone else
on the field, but when he looked out at the
defense all he saw were players who were
bigger and better than he was.

Joey called out the signals and took the
snap. Pablo ran out a few yards then faked
a move to his right and cut back to his left.
The ball was already in the air, but Pablo
had taken too long to do his fake, and he

couldn't catch up to the pass. The pass hit the ground just past his outstretched hands for an incomplete pass.

It's so much easier in practice, Pablo thought as he joined his teammates back in the huddle. "A little faster on the cut," Joey said. "Just like—"

"I know," Pablo interrupted. "Just like in practice."

As the game wore on, Pablo felt himself running crisper pass patterns and using his speed to get open more often. But despite his improved play, Pablo's team trailed 21–10, with just over seven minutes left to play. They had the ball on their own forty-yard line. It was third down and eight yards to go.

"Let's run the down-and-out to Pablo," Joey said in the huddle.

Pablo knew exactly what the play was. He remembered where he had to be and what he had to do. He just had to execute all the right moves. As he lined up, Pablo saw that Ricky, who was faster than Kiesha, was now covering him as the defensive back.

Joey took the snap from Ernie, and Pablo took off quickly from the line. He knew his team needed eight yards to get a first down and keep the drive going. When Pablo was ten yards out from the line of scrimmage he faked sharply to his left.

Ricky went for the fake.

Pablo cut crisply back to the right. The pass was right there. He hauled in the ball for a twelve-yard gain and the first down. Then he stepped out of bounds to stop the clock and give his team more time for their comeback.

The ball sat at midfield as the team huddled up around Joey. "Let's go with a play-action pass. Vicki, the fake hand-off will go to you. Pablo, you run a post pattern.

I'll hit you coming across the middle."

Pablo felt himself getting into a rhythm.
He glanced out at the defense. *Gotta make a
really good cut on this play and just outrun
Ricky to the ball*, he thought as Joey took
the snap.

Joey turned and pretended to hand the
ball off to Vicki. She put her head down and
ran through the line as if she had the ball.

Thinking it was a running play, Ricky
slowed down on defense just in case he had
to back up his linemen and stop Vicki.

This was the advantage Pablo needed. He
cut on an angle toward the goalpost and put
on a burst of speed, gaining a step on Ricky.
As Pablo made his cut, Joey threw a bullet
pass that Pablo caught up to and grabbed.

A.C., a linebacker, was coming toward
Pablo and snatched his flag. But the play
had brought Pablo's team to the thirty-yard
line in enemy territory. Just under five

minutes showed on the clock.

Pablo and his team were rolling.

Joey called a draw play next. The play was set up to fool the defense into thinking he was going to throw a pass, but it was actually a running play.

Pablo knew his job on the play was to run his pattern with the same intensity he would if the play were going to him. Vicki lined up behind Joey in the running-back position.

Ernie snapped the ball and Joey dropped back as if to pass. Vicki stayed in the backfield looking like she was going to help block.

Pablo took off downfield, covered by Ricky. He sped out ten yards, then cut sharply to his left and looked back toward Joey as if he were about to receive a pass. Ricky stayed with him, guarding him tightly. A.C. hurried over to help.

Joey dropped back and stopped next to Vicki. He looked downfield at Pablo, drew back his right arm as if to throw, then handed the ball off to Vicki.

Reese, Dante, and Pete, the defensive linemen, were rushing hard, believing that Joey was going to throw a pass. Vicki took the ball and scooted right past them. She had an open field in front of her.

Vicki dashed right down the middle of the field, crossing the twenty-yard line. Kiesha, now playing linebacker, finally caught up to

the speeding Vicki and grabbed her flag at the fifteen-yard line.

"Okay guys, we've got about four minutes to go and we've got to score two touchdowns," Joey said when his team had gathered in the huddle. "I think it's time to unleash our secret weapon—Pablo's throwing arm! Let's try a reverse play. You remember what we talked about, right, Pabs?"

"Right," Pablo replied. *I know I can do this,* he thought, gritting his teeth. *I can make it happen.*

The team broke the huddle and Pablo lined up on the right side.

Joey took the snap, spun around, and handed the ball off to Vicki. She ran to her right as if she were going to try to run along the sideline.

Pablo, meanwhile, took two quick steps forward, like he was running out for a pass.

Then he stopped suddenly, turned around, and ran toward Vicki in the backfield.

As he passed her, Vicki handed the ball off to Pablo who continued running to his left. As soon as she had given the ball to Pablo, Vicki raced downfield.

Just before Pablo reached the left sideline he stopped. He set himself, drew back his arm, and fired a pass downfield to Vicki.

The defense was so confused by the trick play that Vicki found herself wide open in the end zone. She caught Pablo's pass for a touchdown.

Vicki trotted back and gave Pablo a high five. "Way to go, Pablo," she said. "Who knew that we had two quarterbacks on this team!"

"Joey's still the quarterback, Vicki," Pablo said quickly. "I'm just the secret weapon."

Tony kicked the extra point, then kicked

off. His team still trailed 21–17 with three minutes left to play.

"Okay guys, we need a big stop here," Joey said in the defensive huddle. "We can't let them eat up the clock. We've got to get the ball back one more time to win this thing."

Pablo's success on offense was helping his confidence on defense. On first down, he grabbed Pete's flag on a running play to limit him to a two-yard gain. Then after Ricky threw two incomplete passes, his team was forced to punt.

Pete got off a short punt. A ten-yard runback by Sam put her team just across midfield, forty-five yards from a game-winning touchdown.

Just over two minutes were left in the game.

Joey moved the offense steadily up the field. Short sideline passes to Pablo and to Vicki coming out of the backfield picked up yardage and also stopped the clock. With just twelve seconds remaining, Joey huddled up his team. The ball was on the eighteen-yard line, but they now faced a third-down-and-seven situation.

"I don't think we have time to get a first down here," Joey said. "I think we should go for it all in the end zone."

"Maybe we should try the reverse again," Vicki suggested.

"I don't think so," Joey said. "They'll be looking for that."

Pablo felt relieved. As well as he had done, the last thing he wanted was to be responsible for throwing the pass that could win or lose the game.

"Pablo, I want you to run out about

ten yards, then stop and turn around just like you were running a curl route," Joey explained. "I'll fake it to you. Ricky should step up to go for the stop. That's when you turn back and head for the end zone, where I'll hit you with the game-winning pass."

Pablo took a deep breath and ran through the play in his mind. The final play was still going to come down to him.

As the ball was snapped, Pablo sped off the line. Ricky was with him step for step. A few yards from the end zone Pablo stopped, turned around, and reached out as if he expected to catch the pass right there. Ricky went for the fake. Pablo spun back around, past Ricky, and ran into the end zone. He was open. Now all he had to do was catch the pass.

Joey threw a line-drive spiral right at Pablo.

Pablo felt his heart start to pound. He

was going to do it. He was going to catch the game-winning pass. He was going to be a good football player after all.

The ball hit Pablo's hands, bounced off, and rolled to the ground. Incomplete pass. Game over. Pablo's team had lost 21–17.

Pablo walked slowly off the field with his head hanging down. "I'm so sorry that I let everyone down again!" he said to his teammates. No one said a word, but he could tell that everyone was disappointed. *No one likes to lose,* he thought. *Especially not when the game was right there in my hands.*

Ernie finally spoke up. "Hey, you've been working hard, right?" he asked. "You were studying that playbook so much at lunch the other day you didn't even know I was there."

"I am working hard," Pablo admitted. "But the big plays make me really nervous. I'm so worried I'll mess up that that's exactly what happens."

"There's only one thing to do," Joey said, putting his arm around Pablo's shoulder.

"I know," Pablo said, determined to work even harder. "Keep practicing."

Chapter Five

On the morning of the next team
practice, Pablo was studying his playbook so
intently again that he lost track of the time.
Realizing he was going to be late, he hurried
off to the practice field.

By the time he got to the field, the rest of
the team had gathered. As he approached,
Pablo could hear their conversation. It didn't
take him long to realize that they were
all talking about him. He stopped a short
distance away and listened, not letting on
that he had arrived.

"I know it's not his fault, Joey, and I
would never say anything to Pablo, but that

dropped pass cost us the game," Pablo heard Tony say.

"You're right, Tony," Joey replied. "I wasn't happy about losing either, but it's not like Pablo isn't trying. He's practicing hard. Sometimes even by himself."

"And he's always reading the playbook," Ernie added. "He probably goes to bed with it on his head, hoping that maybe some of it will seep into his brain while he sleeps."

"Then I don't know what his problem is," Vicki said. "Pablo's good at every other sport. And he's working hard at football. So what gives?"

"I don't know, Vicki," Sam said. "I think maybe he's psyching himself out, thinking too much."

Pablo stood silently, taking all this in. *Sam's right,* he thought. *I'm thinking too much, making myself all nervous before a big play. I understand the game now. I've read every play a hundred times. I've run all the pass patterns over and over. Now I just have to trust myself and play the game.*

Waiting for a pause in the conversation, so his friends wouldn't know that he had been listening, Pablo ran onto the field.

"Hey guys," Pablo called out. "What are we standing around yakking for? Let's play some football!"

Joey looked at the others and shrugged. "Okay, Pabs. Why don't you run that play that ended the game?"

"Sure," Pablo replied. *Maybe if I run it enough in practice, I won't get so nervous when I have to run it at crunch time.*

Pablo dashed downfield about ten yards then stopped, turned around, and looked back at Joey. Joey faked a throw. Then Pablo spun back around and continued into the end zone. The ball was right there, and this time Pablo caught it and held on tightly.

"That's the way it's done," Joey shouted.
"Easy as that!"

"Easy as that," Pablo repeated.

"Nice catch, Pablo!" Tony shouted. "Let's
see the ball!"

Pablo reared back and fired a pass. It
arced through the air and landed right in
Tony's hands.

"Nice throw!" Sam said. "We definitely have
to run that reverse again in our next game."

"Good stuff, Pablo!" Ernie cried. "I know
how hard you've been studying."

"I know every play in our playbook," Pablo
said proudly.

The team ran through their usual drills.
They practiced running plays, pass patterns,
and blocking. Pablo felt his confidence grow
with each pass he caught or threw. When the
practice ended, the team did their usual lap
around the field.

"I don't know, Joey," Tony said as he

jogged along. He pointed at Pablo who ran beside him. "This guy here is giving you a run for your money as quarterback."

"No way!" Pablo cried. "I'm not after Joey's job. I'm just glad to be part of this team."

"And I'm just glad you finally learned all the plays in the playbook," Ernie said. "It's boring talking to myself at lunch."

"Yeah, I can see how that would be boring, having talked to you," Vicki joked. She never passed up an opportunity to give Ernie a hard time.

"You ready for our next game, Pabs?" Joey asked.

Pablo flashed him the thumbs-up sign. He was still nervous, but he was determined not to let it get the best of him next time.

Chapter Six

"Huddle up, everyone!" Joey shouted. His team gathered around him. Joey and his friends were playing against Ricky, Pete, and their teammates. Everyone on Joey's team was determined to finally win a game.

But no one was more determined than Pablo.

He and his teammates had marched downfield using short passes and running plays. Pablo caught three passes, beating his man and keeping a firm grip on the football each time.

"Okay, it's second and five," Joey said in the huddle. "We're twenty-five yards from their end zone. They're expecting a running play since we have two shots at getting the first down. But instead—"

"—we're going to fool them with a play-action pass, right, Joey?" Pablo finished Joey's sentence.

"Right!" Joey replied. "You not only throw like a quarterback, Pabs, but you're starting to think like one, too! Play-action pass. Pablo, you run a post pattern. I'll fake the hand-off, then hit you in the end zone."

Joey lined up behind Ernie, with Vicki set up as running back behind him. Pablo ran a few yards to the left and set himself.

On the snap, Joey took the ball, then turned and faked a hand-off to Vicki, who ran into the line as if she had the ball. The defense, already thinking run, went for the fake. This gave Joey plenty of time to set up for the pass.

Pablo, meanwhile, started off his route running less than full speed. He was trying to fool Ricky, who was covering him, into thinking the play really was going to Vicki.

About fifteen yards down the field, Pablo cut toward the goalpost and kicked his legs into high gear, using all his speed. He caught Ricky by surprise.

Joey had plenty of time to throw his pass, which arrived in the end zone at the

same moment as Pablo. Pablo grabbed the pass for the touchdown to give his team the lead. Tony's extra point made the score 7–0.

"You had it all the way, Pabs!" Joey said giving Pablo a high five when he returned to the huddle.

"I know," Pablo said, smiling confidently.

Following the kickoff, Pablo and his teammates set up to play defense.

Ricky, playing quarterback for the other team, started on his own thirty-yard line. He took the snap from A.C. Ricky handed the ball off to Pete, the running back.

Pete burst through the line, following his blockers. As he passed Joey, and was about to break loose for a long gain, Joey turned and dove after him.

Joey extended his body in midair and reached out with his right hand. He just barely managed to snatch the flag from Pete's belt, saving a big play. But as Joey crashed to the ground, he landed on his right wrist.

"Ahhh!" Joey cried out in pain. He clutched his right wrist with his left hand and rolled over onto his back.

All the players from both teams quickly gathered around him.

"Are you okay?" Pete asked.

"I don't know," Joey said as Sam and Pablo helped him to his feet. He tried to bend his wrist and winced. "It's really sore. I don't think it's broken or anything, but it might be sprained."

He hurried over to the sideline and pulled out the team's first aid bag. Ernie wrapped

Joey's wrist with an elastic bandage for support. "Do you think you'll ever play the piano again?" he joked.

Joey laughed and got to his feet. "No worse than I played it before," he replied. "I'm okay. Let's keep playing."

As Joey joined his teammates in the defensive huddle, no one asked the question that was in the front of everyone's mind—
Would Joey be able to throw the ball when his team went back on offense?

With his wrist securely taped he was able to play on the defensive line. He could rush the passer and take the flag from a runner.

But whether or not he could throw the football with an injured wrist was another story.

His teammates didn't have to wait long to find out. On the very next play, Pete fumbled the ball. Ernie recovered the fumble and his team took over thirty yards away from a touchdown.

"Let me try a couple of practice throws," Joey said, taking the ball from Ernie. "Pablo, run a short-out pattern."

Pablo ran out a few yards then cut to the sideline. Joey reached back to throw and dropped the ball to the ground. "Yah!" he cried out. "No way I can throw. I just can't bend the wrist."

"What are we going to do now?" Pablo asked, dreading the answer he expected.

"You are going to fill in as quarterback, Pablo," Joey replied.

"Me?" Pablo cried, feeling his confidence

suddenly drain away. "But I just got comfortable being a wide receiver. You want me to step in as the leader, the field general?"

"Think about it," Joey said softly. "You said yourself that you know every play in our playbook. And you can't deny the fact that you've got a great arm. It's got to be you, Pabs. Either that or we have to forfeit the game."

Pablo knew Joey was right. But he'd never actually played quarterback in a real game. He'd just have to learn as he went. "Okay, Joey," Pablo said anxiously. "I'm the quarterback."

"All right!" Joey cried. "I'd switch positions with you, but I don't think I can catch the ball either."

"I'll take over as wide receiver," Tony volunteered. "Joey, you take my place on the offensive line."

The team huddled around Pablo. He took a deep breath then spoke up. "Running play," he began. "Vicki, you take it between Sam and Ernie on the left side of the line."

Pablo lined up behind the center. Ernie snapped the ball. Pablo turned and handed it off to Vicki. She tried to slip in between Sam and Ernie who were blocking for her.

But Dante charged off the defensive line quickly and grabbed Vicki's flag before she had even gained a yard.

Pablo called for another running play on second down.

As they broke the huddle, Joey thought that Pablo might be hesitating to throw his first pass in a real game. *He* would have called for a pass play on second down. But Pablo was now the quarterback, and the game was in his hands.

The second-down running play had little more success than the first, setting up a third-and-nine situation.

Pablo knew what he had to do. "Tony, let's try a curl pattern," he said. "Make sure you've got the first down before you turn around."

Tony smiled. "I thought you'd never ask," he said as the team broke the huddle.

Pablo took the snap from Ernie and dropped back. He watched as Tony bolted off the line, ran out ten yards, then turned around. Just as Tony started to turn around, Pablo fired the ball.

The pass was straight and true, heading right for Tony, but Ricky, the defensive back had Tony played perfectly. He stepped in front of Tony and intercepted the pass.

Ricky headed upfield. He picked up two key blocks from Pete and Dante, allowing him to race seventy yards for a touchdown. The extra point tied the game at 7–7.

"Let it go, Pabs," Joey said as his team

lined up to receive the kickoff. "It's just one play. You'll get them next time. Right now, just stay focused on the kickoff."

"Okay," Pablo said. He appreciated Joey looking out for him, not giving him a chance to get down on himself.

Dante kicked off. The ball spun, end over end, heading right toward Pablo. He caught it and started running upfield. He passed his own twenty-yard line, then his thirty and forty. As he crossed midfield, Pablo picked up two blockers. Using his great speed, Pablo raced downfield before Kiesha finally grabbed his flag. But his speed and determination had put his team in a great position to score. First and ten, twenty yards from the end zone.

"This time I'm not waiting," Pablo said in the huddle. He was energized by his long runback. "Let's take back the lead."

Pablo called for Tony to run a straight

fly-pattern into the end zone. Nothing fancy. He'd just have to outrun Ricky, and Pablo would have to make sure the ball was in exactly the right spot.

Pablo took the snap and dropped back. Tony sped downfield. Ricky tried to stay with him, but Tony kept one step ahead the whole way.

Just before Tony crossed into the end zone, Pablo fired a long arcing pass downfield. The ball soared past Ricky's outstretched hands. Tony looked back over his shoulder and reached out for the pass, but the ball was about a foot out of his reach. It bounced into the back of the end zone.

Pablo turned away in frustration. *I know I can do this. I just have to do it!*

"Let's go guys," Joey said, trying to keep everyone's spirit up. "Second down. Let's get in this time."

Pablo was finding it harder and harder to focus. He attempted two more passes, but each time he overthrew or underthrew the receiver. On fourth down, his team had to settle for a field goal. Tony's kick was true and gave his team a 10–7 lead.

But Pablo knew it would have been 14–7 if he had just thrown one of those passes the way he should have.

Following the kickoff, Ricky led his team on a long drive, which ate up lots of time. He hit Dante on a slant pattern in the end zone to regain the lead, 14–10.

After the kickoff, before they joined their teammates in the huddle, Joey pulled Pablo aside. "Remember, Pabs, it's only you and the receiver out there," Joey said. "Forget about everyone else. Just focus on Tony. You make those passes every time in practice. It's no different here."

Pablo knew Joey was right.

His team trailed 14–10 as he broke the huddle. Time was winding down with about five minutes left to play and seventy yards to go to take back the lead.

Pablo called for a play-action pass. He took the snap, then turned and faked a hand-off to Vicki. Looking downfield, he focused only on Tony, who dashed twelve yards then cut toward the sideline. Pablo fired a perfect spiral that Tony caught just

before he stepped out of bounds to stop the clock.

Finally! Pablo thought. *A completed pass. And I stopped the clock, too.* He breathed a small sigh of relief.

"Perfect throw!" Tony cried, giving Pablo a high five as he returned to the huddle. "What's next?"

"Okay, Tony, I want you to run out about ten yards, then stop and turn around just like you were running a curl route," Pablo said. "I'll fake it to you. When Ricky steps up, you turn back and head upfield."

"Awesome," Tony said as the team broke the huddle.

Despite the fact that his wrist still hurt, Joey smiled to himself as he took his position on the offensive line. He realized that Pablo had just called the same play in which he had dropped what would have been the game-winning pass in their last game. That alone told him that Pablo was finally really in the game.

Pablo took the snap, dropped back, and watched as Tony broke hard from the line of scrimmage, then stopped and turned back. Pablo faked a throw. Just as he had hoped, Ricky stepped around Tony, hoping for another interception.

Tony turned back upfield and took off. Leading him perfectly, Pablo's pass floated into Tony's hands. He dashed down the sideline, eating up yardage.

"Go Tony!" Pablo shouted, waving his arms to urge Tony on.

Kiesha finally caught up to Tony and grabbed his flag as he crossed her team's twenty-yard line. Two minutes remained.

"Here's where we win this ball game," Tony said, clapping his hands as he returned to the huddle.

Pablo called two pass plays, trying to

hit Tony in the end zone each time. But the defense tightened up, desperately trying to hold onto their lead. They deflected both passes.

Down by four points, Pablo knew that a field goal wasn't an option. He had to score a touchdown.

"I think it's time for a gadget play," Pablo announced to his teammates in the huddle. He had run through every play in the playbook in his mind and believed he had picked the perfect one.

"That reverse worked when you were the wide receiver," Tony pointed out. "But I can't throw like you do!"

"That's not the play I have in mind," Pablo said. "We're going to run the flea flicker. Vicki, Tony, I'll need you both on this one. It's got to look like a reverse, with one more twist." Then Pablo outlined to his teammates what he hoped would be the game-winning play.

Pablo brought his team up to the line. Tony set up wide to the right. Vicki lined up behind Pablo, a few steps to his left.

Pablo called out signals in a strong, confident voice. "Green-31-green-31. Hut-hut!"

Ernie snapped the ball. Pablo spun around and handed it off to Vicki who was running hard to her right. As soon as the hand-off was complete, Tony, rather than run downfield as usual, turned back and headed to his left, still in the backfield.

Vicki handed the ball off to Tony who ran past Pablo, sweeping around to the left side of the field. It looked just like the reverse play Pablo had run when he was the receiver. But one more surprise was still to come.

Just before he crossed the line of scrimmage, Tony turned and tossed a lateral pass back to Pablo. Pablo looked downfield and saw Vicki racing to the end zone. He threw a high arcing pass.

Vicki crossed into the end zone just as the ball left Pablo's hand. Ricky had been fooled on the play, but A.C. and Kiesha had picked up Vicki as she ran downfield. All three of them leaped into the air at the same time. But Pablo had placed the ball perfectly, just out of reach of the two defenders. At the top of her jump, Vicki caught the ball and came down in the end zone for a touchdown.

Pablo raced downfield and gave Vicki a high five. "What a catch!" he shouted.

"Pretty good throw, too!" Vicki replied.

"Excuse me, can I have your autograph?" Ernie joked as he ran up to Pablo.

Joey caught up to Pablo and offered him a high five—with his left hand.

Tony kicked the extra point to give his team a 17–14 lead. Less than a minute remained. After the kickoff, the defense made three straight stops. Then, on the final play of the game, Pablo swatted away a pass just as time ran out.

Ricky and his teammates exchanged high fives with Pablo and his friends.

"I don't know, Joey," Ricky said. "You may have just lost your job as starting quarterback."

"Ricky's right," Joey said, looking right at Pablo. "I may have to battle you for the starting job once my wrist heals."

Pablo smiled at Joey. "If you like," he said. "I can give you a couple of pointers!"